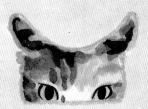

My cat is very independent.

She doesn't come when I call her,
and she runs away if I try to hug her.
She never looks me in the eye.

But if I pretend I don't see her,
or if I walk away,
then she'll follow me and try to play.
And then, my cat copies me.

Kane/Miller Book Publishers, Inc.
First American Edition 2007
by Kane/Miller Book Publishers, Inc.
La Jolla, California

All rights reserved. For information contact:
Kane/Miller Book Publishers, Inc.
P.O. Box 8515
La Jolla, CA 92038
www.kanemiller.com

Library of Congress Control Number: 2006931559
Printed and bound in China

1 2 3 4 5 6 7 8 9 10

ISBN: 978-1-933605-26-5

My Cat Copies Me

Yoon-duck Kwon

Kane/Miller
BOOK PUBLISHERS

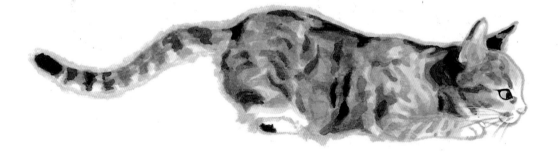

My cat copies me. We tunnel under newspapers,

and crouch behind doors.

If I hide under the desk,

or in the closet, she hides with me.

My cat copies me. We help with the laundry,

and chase after flies.

Smelling the flowers,

or watching bugs, she always copies me.

When we are tired of playing, we sit together.

My cat is my best friend, and I am hers.

At nighttime, we prick up our ears, and listen. Is Mommy home?

When I get scared, I hide under my
blanket, and my cat hides with me.
She snuggles in, and purrs.
My friend, my cat, copies me.

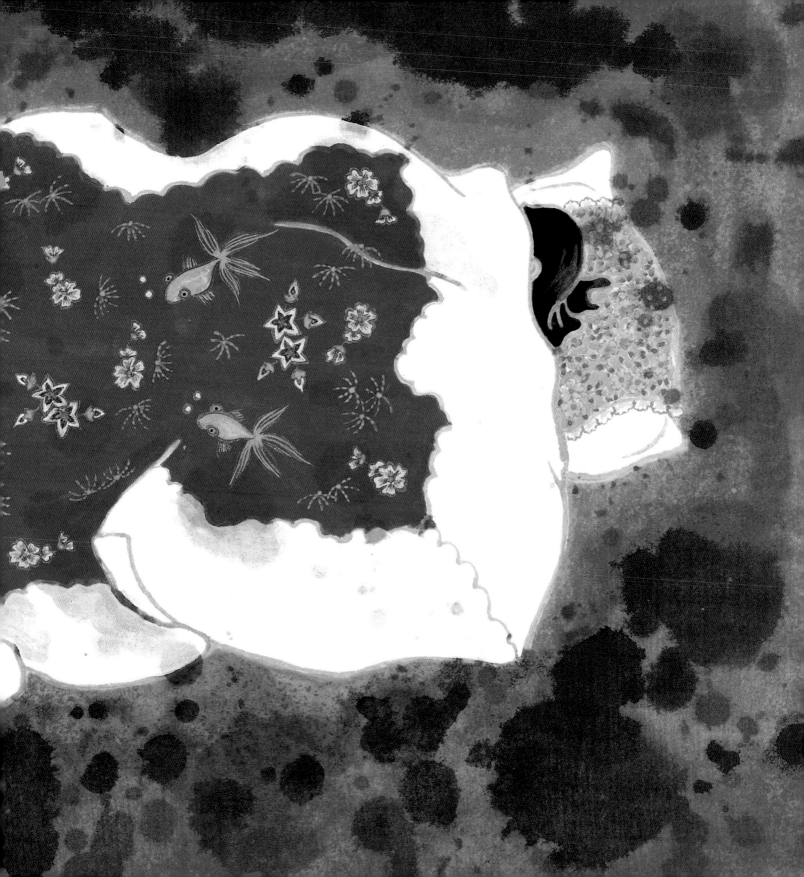

But from now on…

...I will copy my cat!

Like my cat, I'll look outside.
I'll watch the darkness, and I won't be afraid.

Like my cat, I'll climb high,
and see things far away.
Everything will look different.
Everything will be different.

Like my cat, I'll stretch my body.
(I'll stretch my mind, too.)
I won't be scared of anything!

We'll go outside, together!
We'll make new friends, together!